Ingrid and Dieter Schubert

THERE'S A CROCODILE
UNDER MY BED!

McGraw-Hill Book Company

NEW YORK   ST. LOUIS   SAN FRANCISCO

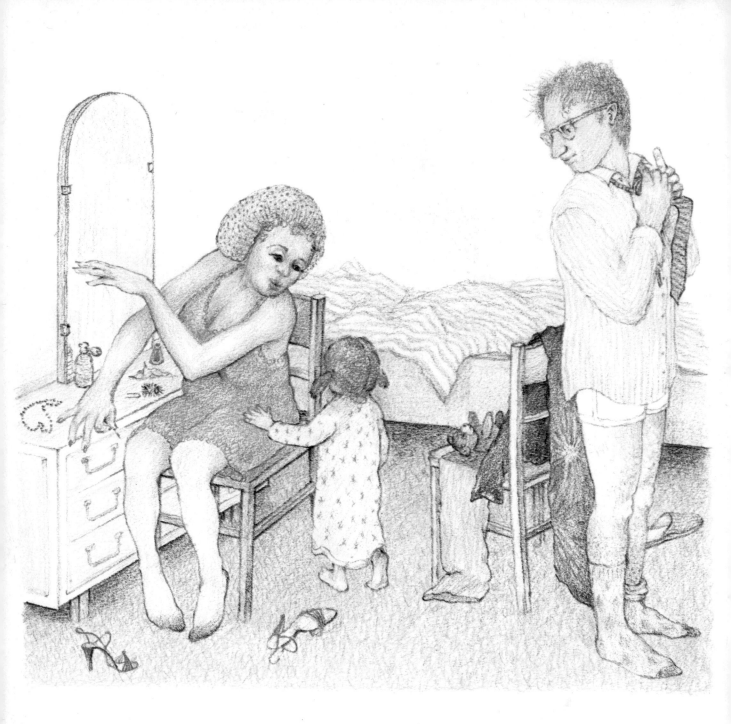

I T WAS JUST SEVEN O'CLOCK: bedtime for Peggy. Her parents
were going out, so there was no time for chatting or for reading a
story. Mama was polishing her fingernails as Peggy kissed her good night.
  Papa said: "Now off to bed, Peggy!"

Peggy grabbed her bear and danced down the hall. She opened her bedroom door and… she couldn't believe her eyes. Under her bed was a CROCODILE, his big eyes shining in the lamplight!

Peggy banged the door shut and raced back to her parents.

"I can't go to sleep!" she cried. "There's a crocodile under my bed!"

Mama sighed. Papa picked Peggy up and carried her back to her room. He opened the door, and there was no crocodile to be seen.

"You see, Peggy, there is no crocodile. Not under the blankets and not under the bed." He turned the bed covers back and crawled under the bed for proof before going on. "Just a lot of rubbish, shoes and toys and things. Besides, crocodiles are too big to hide under beds. You can find them only in the Zoo and in places like Africa."

After tucking Peggy into bed, he said: "Now go to sleep and not another word from you!"

Papa had hardly put out the light, when Peggy heard some giggling. Where was it coming from?, she wondered. She looked under the bed and at the bookshelf.

"Hello! I'm up here!" a deep, hoarse voice called. On top of the wardrobe a huge crocodile was crouched, looking down on Peggy in a teasing sort of way.

Peggy just gasped, "Go away, you scare me!"

"There is nothing to be afraid of," the crocodile replied as he jumped down from the wardrobe. "My name is James and I am a very unusual crocodile. Just watch!"

Peggy's eyes grew round as saucers as the crocodile shrank and shrank until he was about the size of Peggy's sneaker.

"Do you like me better this way?" he chirped.

Peggy thought, and then she answered, "No, I prefer you big—I don't think I feel scared anymore."

"As you wish," said the crocodile, coming back to his normal size before he sat down on the bed.

"Where did you come from?" Peggy asked him.

"From the Land of Crocodiles. But that is a long story that I may tell you later. First I would like to wash as I am very dusty."

Peggy took James by the paw and led him to the bathroom. She prepared his bath (with plenty of her mother's shampoo), and James slid into it, grunting with pleasure.

"This is lovely! Why don't you join me, little one?" he invited her.

With hats of shampoo they played together in the bathtub.

Peggy, the sea monster, threatened the dolls and boats, and James, the hero, saved them by swishing them over the side with his tail.

When the water grew colder, Peggy showed James how she could keep her head underwater for quite a long time.

James was impressed.

Finally they dried themselves off and went into the living room.

"If we can have music," James told her, "I'll show you the Crocodile-Rock!"

Peggy put a record on the stereo, and James was off!

The Crocodile-Rock was terrific! James moved smoothly like a
ballroom dancer, then stood on his front paws tapping time against
the ceiling with his tail.

He tossed Peggy in the air, making her turn around three times
before she landed in his paws again. In the end they were
both out of breath.

"What shall we do next?" Peggy
asked after they had rested.
    "Let's make a crocodile!" James
suggested. "A tiny one."

James told her what they would
need, and Peggy found two egg
cartons, a large one and a small one.
And green paint, and red paint, and
brushes and white paper, and
scissors and a lot of glue.

They glued the top and the
bottom of the large box together—
that made the body. They cut
terrible white teeth from the paper,
and they painted the small eggbox
red inside! That made the head. A
paper tail was glued to one end, and
the boxes were painted all green
outside except for two very fierce
red eyes.

James tied the head to the body:
the crocodile was ready! It looked
much more frightening than James!

Suddenly Peggy began to yawn. She couldn't stop.

"You should go to sleep," said James, and he carried her to bed.

"But you promised to tell me about the Land of Crocodiles, and why you are here, James," she reminded him.

"Yes, of course!" He made himself comfortable at the end of the bed and began: "Now the LAND OF CROCODILES is a beautiful country and very warm. But it is not for crocodiles only. There are elephants and hippopotami and pelicans and ostriches, tortoises, giraffes, and many other animals.

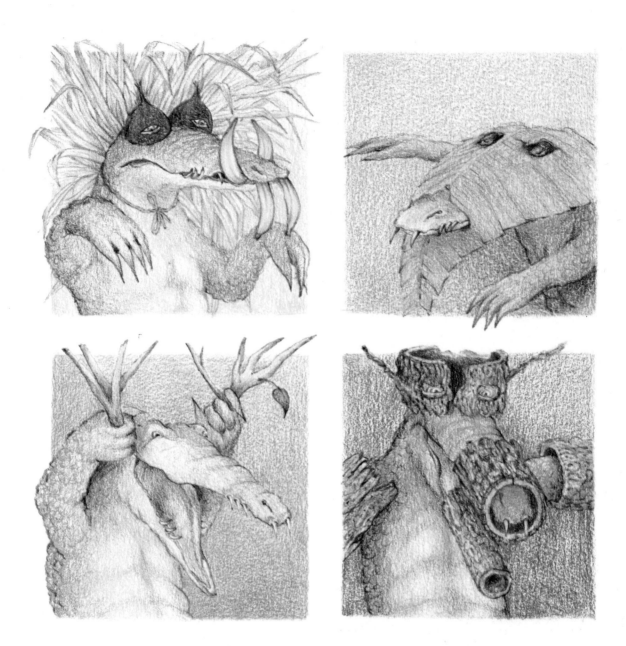

"I was young and did a lot of mischief. Most of all I loved to frighten the small ones. I told them creepy stories just before dark, about ghosts and witches and monsters, so the poor things did not dare to go to sleep. Or I disguised myself as a terrible ogre with horns or a snout ready to swallow the young. One day I scared them all away by popping up in the river with long hair like a seawitch.

"After that I had a very wicked idea: I exchanged the crocodile eggs for ostrich eggs. When the eggs hatched the turmoil was terrible. The crocodiles and the ostriches didn't know what had happened to their young.

"The baby crocodiles had feathers, and the baby ostriches had tough skins and they made for the water at once.

"The older animals were furious and decided to put a stop to my mischief: I was summoned to appear before the Council of the Seven Wise Crocodiles.

"There I stood all alone while the animals complained in turn about my little jokes. That took quite a long time. In the end the eldest of the Wise Crocodiles addressed me:

'You have annoyed and frightened the young so much that no animal child dares to go to sleep alone. You have done that day after day, and your tricks have become ever more sickening. Finally, you have exchanged eggs and have caused great grief to the parents: the ostriches who saw their brood take to the water, and the crocodiles who saw their young run on long legs. You must learn to be nice to the young and stop frightening them.

'Therefore, we are sending you to the Land of Man. There, many children are afraid of the dark. You must learn to comfort them and to make them forget their fears. To help you in your task you shall have two gifts: you will speak the language of man and you will be able to make yourself quite small so as not to scare the children of man.

'When in this way you have given love and comfort to a thousand children, you may return to us.

'Will you promise to be nice to the children of man?'

"I promised solemnly. Then the wise old crocodile made me drink something that sent me off to sleep at once.

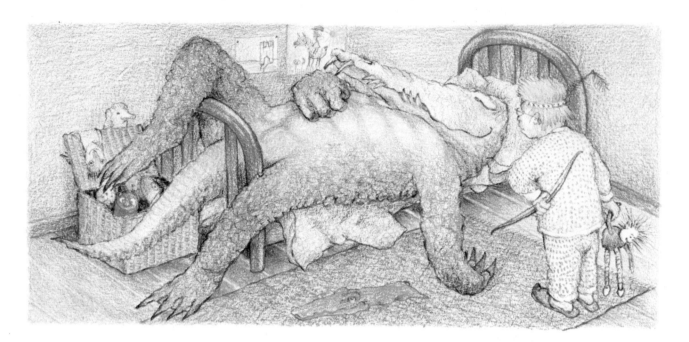

"When I woke up I found myself in the bed of a small boy.
Somehow he wasn't afraid. At first I didn't know what to say or
do. We just smiled, and in the end we spent a very nice evening
together, playing cowboys and Indians.

"That was my first visit. Since then I have visited hundreds of
children and I feel quite at home now with the children of man.
You, Peggy, are the nine-hundred-ninety-ninth. Tomorrow, I hope
to see my thousandth child. After that I will return to the Land of
Crocodiles—but from time to time I will come back to visit you and
other children of man."

Peggy was asleep before James had finished the story.
He gently pulled the bed clothes up around
her, turned off the light, and left the room.

The next morning, when Peggy's mother pulled the curtains aside, a ray of sunlight fell under the bed, directly onto the eggbox-crocodile.

"So there was a crocodile under your bed after all!" cried her father in surprise.

Peggy just smiled.